Horse in the House

Other titles in the bunch:

Baby Bear Comes Home
Big Dog and Little Dog Visit the Moon
Delilah Digs for Treasure Dilly and the Goody-Goody
Horse in the House I Don't Want to Say Yes!
Juggling with Jeremy Keeping Secrets
Mabel and Max Magnificent Mummies
Midnight at Memphis Mouse Flute
The Nut Map Owl in the House
Riff-Raff Rabbit Rosie and the Robbers
Runaway Fred Tom's Hats

First published in Great Britain 1998 by Mammoth
an imprint of Reed International Books Ltd
Michelin House, 81 Fulham Rd, London SW3 6RB.
Published in hardback by Heinemann Educational Publishers,
a division of Reed Educational and Professional Publishing Limited
by arrangement with Reed International Books Ltd.
Text Copyright © Brian Morse 1998
Illustrations Copyright © Nick Sharratt 1998
The Author and Illustrator have asserted their moral rights
Paperback ISBN 0 7497 2813 2
Hardback ISBN 0 434 97653 9
10 9 8 7 6 5 4 3 2
A CIP catalogue record for this title is available from the British Library
Printed and bound in Italy by Olivotto

Brian Morse

Horse in the House

Illustrated by Nick Sharratt

BLue Bananas

For my Granddaughter, Elysha
B.M.

For Tim, Jacqueline and Holly
N.S.

Sarah was looking out

of the kitchen window.

Dad was washing up.

'Dad! There's something

in the garden that shouldn't

be there!' Sarah said.

'What's that?' asked Dad,

without looking up.

'It's a horse,'

said Sarah.

'A horse!' Dad said.

'Whatever next.'

'But there really is a horse, Dad,'
said Sarah. 'And it's eating your flowers.'
'Are you sure it's not an elephant
like last time?' said Dad.

And he dried his hands

and walked out of the kitchen.

When Dad had gone upstairs, Sarah opened the door and spoke to the horse.

'Go away! You're not supposed to come
in our garden.'

clip clop

'Oh, no!' said Sarah.

'I didn't mean you to come in.'

13

'Who are you talking to?'
Dad called from the top of the
stairs. 'Is there someone at the door?'

'It's only the horse!' Sarah shouted.

'That's all right, then,' said Dad. 'Are you coming to help me tidy up?'

The horse looked round the kitchen.

It spotted the fruit bowl and helped

itself to a crunchy green apple.

Then it took a red one and knocked

the bowl onto the floor.

bump
thump

'Greedy thing!' Sarah said, picking up the fruit bowl. But the horse took no notice. It munched its way through the apples and then tried an orange. It didn't like the orange, so it spat it on the floor.

19

'Come on, Sarah. Where are you?'

Dad called.

'But Dad, there's . . .' Sarah started to say.

'I know,' Dad said. 'A horse! Just leave it and come and help me to change our big bed. I've finished yours.'

Sarah ran

upstairs. The horse

clumped up behind her.

The horse saw Dad in the big
bedroom and quickly
slipped into Sarah's room.

It looked out of the window and let out a

long breath through its nose.

Snort!

'You're not being very helpful this morning,' Dad said.

Sarah sighed. 'Sorry, Dad,' she said, and she put Mum's pillow straight and helped to pull up the covers.

'Now for job number three,' Dad said.

'What's that?' asked Sarah.

'Hoovering the living room,'

said Dad. 'Are you going

to stay in your bedroom?'

'No!' said Sarah. 'My bedroom's full of . . .'

'Horse! I forgot,' Dad said.

When Sarah heard the buzz of the hoover
downstairs, she went into her room.
The horse was dancing on the rugs,
making them into an untidy heap.

You'll get me into terrible trouble!

'Now what are you
doing?' Sarah asked.
But the horse took no notice.

Next the horse walked across the landing
and into Mum and Dad's room.

Then it lay down on the bed,

as if to see how comfortable it was!

The horse rolled on its back and waved its hooves in the air.

It swished its tail knocking Sarah's mother's perfume bottles from the dressing table.

Sarah flounced

out of the room

and clumped

down the stairs.

Dad had almost finished the hoovering.

'Dad, when you were in your bedroom,

the horse went . . .' Sarah began.

'Mmm,' Dad said.

'Never mind,' said Sarah.

She could see Dad wasn't listening.

Dad went into the kitchen.

'SARAH - where have all the

apples gone?' he yelled.

'And what's this mess on the floor?'

'It was the horse,' said Sarah. 'He ate
all the fruit.'

Dad looked cross as he started to clear up. He put the orange in the bin and wiped the floor.

'Now I'm going outside,' he said,

'to do some gardening.'

As soon as Dad had gone, the horse
came back downstairs. It neighed loudly.
Sarah covered her ears.

'Dad's in the back garden,'
Sarah said. 'You'd better go
out through the front door.'

The horse cantered down
the path, jumped over
the gate and galloped
out of sight.

clip
clop

Dad came rushing round the side of the house. 'I thought I heard a horse galloping by,' he said. 'And something has ruined my roses!'

Sarah sighed.

'I expect you were just imagining the horse, Dad,' she said.

Then she went back inside to
tidy up the bedrooms
before Mum came in.

What
a day!

At least the horse hadn't made as much
mess as the gorilla had yesterday or the
hippopotamus the day before!